Boo to the Who in the Dark!

For Cloudy and Cami – J.D.
For Peter – S.M.

Scholastic Children's Books
Commonwealth House, 1-19 New Oxford Street
London WC1A 1NU, UK
a division of Scholastic Ltd
London ~ New York ~ Toronto ~ Sydney ~ Auckland
Mexico City ~ New Delhi ~ Hong Kong

First published in hardback in the UK by Scholastic Ltd, 2004
First published in paperback in the UK by Scholastic Ltd, 2004
This paperback edition first published in the UK by Scholastic Ltd, 2005

Text copyright © Joyce Dunbar, 2004
Illustrations copyright © Sarah Massini, 2004

ISBN 0 439 96836 4

Printed in Singapore

2 4 6 8 10 9 7 5 3 1

The rights of Joyce Dunbar and Sarah Massini to be identified as the author and illustrator
respectively of this work have been asserted by them in accordance with
the Copyright, Designs and Patents Act, 1988.

Boo to the Who in the Dark!

Joyce Dunbar & Sarah Massini

Hippo

On one side of the wood lived Long-Nose.

On the other side of the wood lived Little-Legs.

Most days they would meet in the middle
of the wood and play together.

They splashed in the river.

They climbed up
the trees.

They played hide-and-seek down the rabbit holes.

They were truly the best of friends.

But there was just one
problem . . . the DARK!
The great big dark that filled
the wood at night.

Long-Nose especially was so afraid of the dark that,
on the short days of winter, no sooner had he rushed out
to meet Little-Legs, than he would scurry back home
again to catch the last of the light.

One day Little-Legs said to Long-Nose,
"What is it about the dark that's so scary?"
"The WHO," said Long-Nose.
"The what?" said Little-Legs.

"The WHO! There's a WHO in the dark that scares me."
"Have you ever seen this WHO?" asked Little-Legs.
"No, but I know it's there."

"Where?"

"In the DARKEST bit of the dark."

"And what does it do?"

"It grabs you.

And gobbles you.

And you can't move,"

shuddered Long-Nose.

"You know what I think?" said Little-Legs, who was the braver of the two. "I think we should go and find this WHO in the dark. I think we should go right up to it and show it we're not scared. I think we should say BOO to the WHO in the DARK."

"You do?" said Long-Nose.
"I do," said Little-Legs.
"But I'm scared," said Long-Nose.
"So am I," said Little-Legs, "but let's do it all the same."

That evening, instead of going home in the daylight, Little-Legs and Long-Nose stayed together in the middle of the wood, waiting for the dark, waiting for the WHO in the dark. "Is this the dark?" asked Little-Legs.

"No," said Long-Nose. "I can still see the leaves in the starshine and the whites of your eyes."
So they waited a bit longer.

"Is this the dark?" asked Little-Legs.
"No," said Long-Nose. "I can still see the path
in the moonlight and the sparkle of your teeth."
So they waited a while longer.

"Is this the dark?" asked Little-Legs.
But before Long-Nose had time to answer, the moon
was blotted out by a cloud. The stars blinked shut.

It was
DARK.

Very DARK.

As DARK as DARK can be.

And then, suddenly. . .

Something grabbed hold of Long-Nose by the nose.
"HELP!" called Long-Nose. "The WHO in the DARK
is pinching my nose! It has big rolling eye-whites!"

Something grabbed hold of Little-Legs by the legs.
"HELP!" cried Little-Legs. "The WHO in the DARK
is hanging on to my legs! It has sharp glittery teeth!"

"I'm being squeezed to a squiggle!" cried Long-Nose.
"I'm being pinched to a puddle!" cried Little-Legs.

"BOO!" yelled Little-Legs.
"SHOO!" shouted Long-Nose.

Suddenly the moon came up and Long-Nose
saw what had grabbed hold of him.
It was Little-Legs!

And Little-Legs saw what had grabbed hold of her.
It was Long-Nose!

Long-Nose
laughed.
Little-Legs
danced.
Together they
chanted,
"BOO
to the
WHO!
SHOO
to the
WHO!
It was only
YOU
in the
DARK!"

But from the top of
the tree, Owl hooted,
"Me too! Me too!"